ISABELLA WOOLY BEAR TIGER MOTH

By Carol Cornelius

Illustrated by
Franz Altschuler

THE CHILD'S WORLD

ELGIN, ILLINOIS 60120

Library of Congress Cataloging in Publication Data

Cornelius, Carol, 1942-
  Isabella Wooly Bear Tiger Moth.

  (A Concept book)
  SUMMARY: A wooly little caterpillar metamor-
phosizes into a beautiful tiger moth.
  [1. Metamorphosis—Fiction] I. Altschuler,
Franz. II. Title
PZ10.3.C81571S   [E]   77-28423
ISBN 0-913778-97-4

Distributed by Childrens Press, 1224 West Van Buren Street, Chicago,
Illinois 60607.

© 1978 The Child's World, Inc.

ISABELLA WOOLY BEAR TIGER MOTH

A tiny caterpillar was coming out of a tiny, round egg. She was the last caterpillar to hatch from the dozens of eggs glued to the mullen leaf.

The eggs were stuck to the leaf so well that, no matter what, they would not roll off. Even the strong winds could not blow them away.

The tiny caterpillar was very hungry. She took a big bite of the leaf. It was not the right taste, so she humped down the leaf to find something better.

She took tasting bites of several other plants
before she found one that had just the right
flavor. It was a large plantain.

The tiny caterpillar started up the leaf, eating all the way. All day, the little caterpillar ate plantain.

When the sun went down, and the air
became cool, she came down the plantain to look
for a leaf to sleep under.

9

In the early morning, the little caterpillar went looking for the plantain again. Along a narrow space, she brushed close to a green, spotted caterpillar. As soon as they started to pass, the light green caterpillar started to giggle.

"He, he! Wooly Bear! Oh! You tickle, Wooly Bear! He, he! Ha, ha, ha!"

The little caterpillar stopped and directed her twelve eyes (six on each side of her head) down the length of her furry brown body. She couldn't see far, even with twelve eyes, but she could see the tip of her tail. It, too, was furry.

"I am awfully hairy," said the little caterpillar. "I really am a Wooly Bear! I'm hungry too!" She hurried on.

All of Wooly Bear's eyes can't
be seen in this picture.

Wooly Bear was getting larger every day,
what with all the plantain she ate. One day, right
in the middle of a big juicy bite, she felt a
strange sensation down her back. Her outer skin
had gotten too tight, and now it was splitting.

"My, that feels better!" said Wooly Bear.
"I have been so uncomfortable!"

She pulled herself out of her outgrown coat
and crawled slowly along the leaf, leaving the
old skin behind.

Now that Wooly Bear was getting so much bigger, it was much easier for hungry birds to see her. One day, while she was crawling along, she noticed a dark shadow over her.

Wooly Bear was so startled that she dropped right off the plantain leaf and rolled into a furry ball.

17

It was a fortunate fall, for the shadow over
Wooly Bear was a big starling, who really liked
eating caterpillars He looked for Wooly Bear,
but couldn't find her. For, when she had curled
up, she had rolled under a leaf.

19

In the days when the air was nippy and
the leaves were starting to rustle, Wooly Bear
decided to travel.

Wooly Bear had gone quite a way, when she
came to a great, huge, wide-open space. It was
really a super-highway with cars and trucks
whizzing up and down. Wooly Bear hurried
along with plantain on her mind.

When she was halfway across the highway, the wheel of a big grain truck came very close to crushing Wooly Bear. The rush of air from the big truck blew her up into the air. . .

and tumbled her across the highway to the other
side. Wooly Bear found such strenuous travel
very tiring.

Wooly Bear crawled into a rusted tin can and fell asleep. This time she slept for many days before the warm sun woke her. Then she nibbled on a little bit of plantain. Soon she was asleep again.

Wooly Bear spent most of the winter curled up in a ball, asleep. Only the warmest sunshiny days could bring her out to eat.

2091054

25

Spring came, and the plantain grew green and tender. Wooly Bear loved the warm sun and fresh plantain. She grew fatter and furrier.

One day, although the sun was shining and even the ground was warm, Wooly Bear began to feel sleepy. She crawled into a crack and began spinning a soft blanket around herself.

Inside the soft cocoon blanket, Wooly Bear grew still. She began to change.

A few days later, when Wooly Bear pushed her way out of the cocoon, she was indeed different. Wooly Bear wasn't Wooly Bear anymore!

She had two beautiful dark-yellow forewings with a dark spot in the middle of each.

She had two beautiful pinkish-yellow hindwings with black specks. Her body was golden brown with three rows of neat black spots.

"I really need a new name," she thought. "Wooly Bear was a very good name when I was a furry caterpillar. But now I am a beautiful moth.

"Isabella Tiger Moth is a beautiful name," she thought. "That's who I am." And she spread her wings to dry.